HUES and HARMONY
(How the Rainbow Butterfly Got Her Colors)

Written by

Marissa Bañez

Illustrated by
Enroc Illustrations
Based on Original Drawings by
Marissa Bañez

In a special place called
	The Beautiful Garden,
		there once lived a
			gray caterpillar.

Because The Beautiful Garden
was filled with bright colors,
the gray caterpillar felt her color was boring and dull
...like she didn't belong.

Sometimes, she cried about it,
making everything in the Beautiful Garden
cry along with her.

But she could sing like crystal bells ringing.

When she sang, no one saw her color because there was nothing boring or dull about her singing.

Her singing made everything in the
Beautiful Garden even more beautiful and brilliant.

And everyone loved her.

Still, she sometimes felt alone.

      So, one day, she decided to go
         where her parents came from to see if she could find out more about herself.

To get there,
        she had to travel
               through different places...

The first place was

The Land of Yellow and Blue,

where the squareheads live.

The caterpillar saw that the

yellow squareheads were sunny and

the blue ones were gloomy.

Still, they got along with each other

because . . .

THEY WERE ALL
SQUAREHEADS!!!

Then,

the caterpillar saw others of a different color!

"They're our beloved children,"

the squareheads explained.

So, the caterpillar sang a song for them:

> We're from The Land of *Yellow* and *Blue*,
> Where our parents' love is true.
> You can easily see what we mean
> As some of us are *green*.

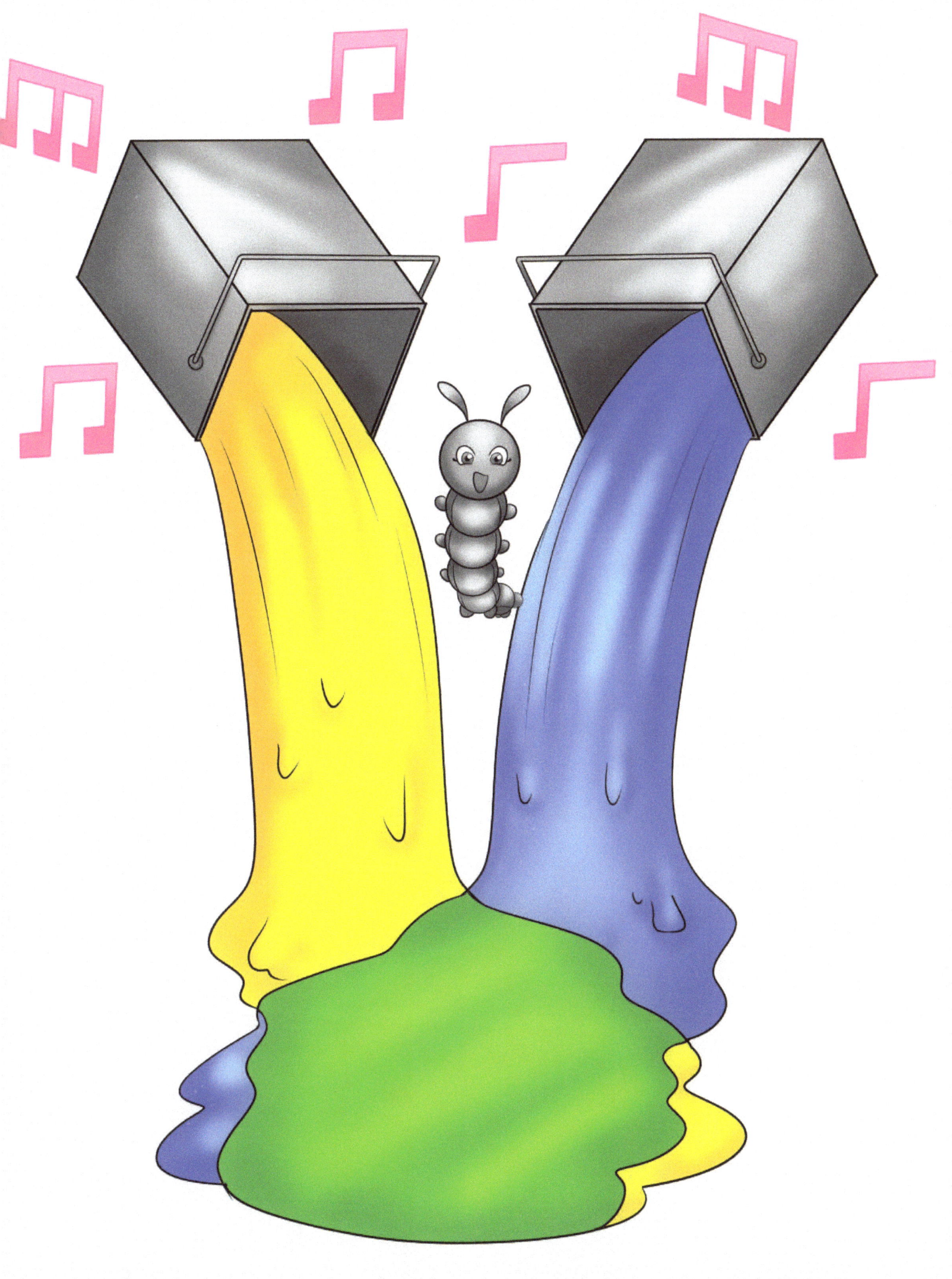

The squareheads were grateful
and made the caterpillar an honorary citizen.

(That's why there are so many
green caterpillars these days.)

The next place was

The Land of Red and Yellow,

where the triangleheads live.

The caterpillar couldn't understand how the

cheerful yellow triangleheads could live with the

mean-looking red triangleheads but they somehow

lived in peace

because...

THEY WERE ALL
TRIANGLEHEADS!!!

The caterpillar soon learned

the red triangleheads weren't mean at all.

When the caterpillar saw a baby

being cared for by his red daddy, she

understood they were just always thinking

about making their children safe and healthy.

So, the caterpillar sang a lullaby for the baby:

We're from The Land of Red and Yellow.
Our parents' love makes us cool and mellow.
Some may say that orange is bright
But for us, it's just right.

To this day,
    all the trianglehead parents
        sing that lullaby to their babies.

Then came
The Land of Red and Blue,
where the trapezoidheads live.

The caterpillar wondered if the red trapezoidheads were angry because the blue trapezoidheads were sad

or

if it was the other way around –
the blues were sad because the reds were angry.

But the caterpillar soon learned no one was angry or sad.
Instead, they always treated each other with dignity like
they were all kings and queens
because . . .

THEY WERE ALL TRAPEZOIDHEADS!!!

So,

    the caterpillar wasn't surprised to see

        that some of the children were the

            majestic color of

                purple.

The caterpillar sang:

We're from The Land of Red and Blue.
Our parents love us through and through.
Mix red and blue, and what do you get?
Purple or violet.

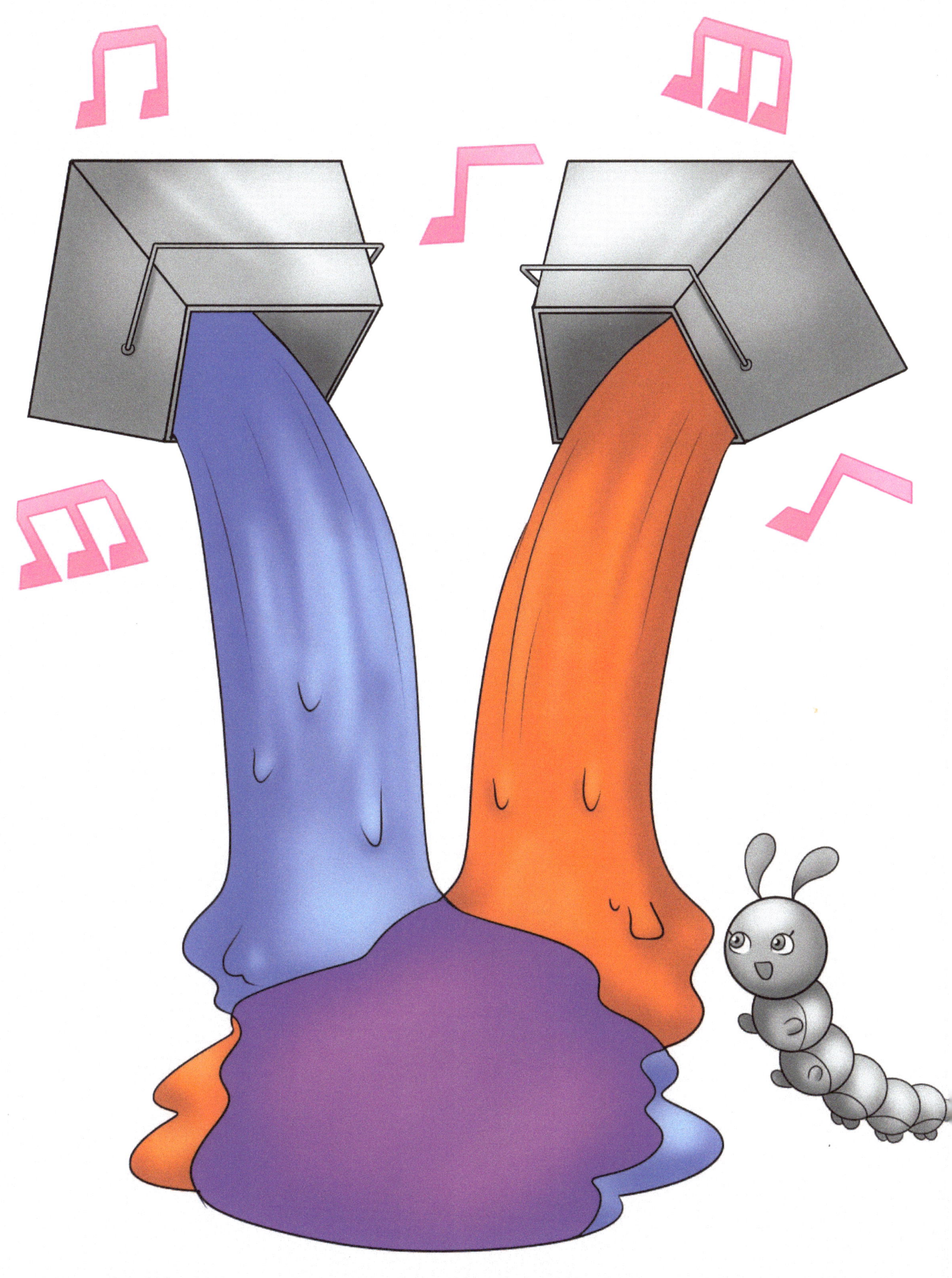

Before the caterpillar left,
the trapezoidheads gave a
big fancy royal banquet
in her honor.

Finally, the caterpillar reached her parents' home:

The Land of Black and White,

where the circleheads live.

The caterpillar saw everyone treating each
other with respect as equals
because...

THEY WERE ALL CIRCLEHEADS!!!

When the caterpillar told them
why she came back, all the circleheads
explained the true meaning of her color:

Gray

represents her parents' love

for each other

and

for her.

To honor her parents,

she sang a song with all her love:

We're from The Land of Black and White,
With just shades of dark and light.
Our parents' love is here to stay
'Cause some of us are gray.

Everyone in
The Land of Black and White
agreed to make the caterpillar's song their
national anthem.

While the caterpillar was away,

very special fairies from the nearby

Fabled Fairy Forest and their butterfly-loving

friend Esperanza built a chrysalis in

The Beautiful Garden.

It was made of the finest gold.

The fairies and Esperanza made this type of

chrysalis only for caterpillars who learned

something very important that had to be shared with

the world when they became butterflies.

When the caterpillar returned to

The Beautiful Garden,

she was very tired and was thankful for the chrysalis,

where she could finally rest.

As the caterpillar entered the gold chrysalis, a

brilliant rainbow suddenly appeared and

landed on the chrysalis.

After

a

couple

of

weeks,

the

chrysalis

c-r-a-c-k-e-d

open...

In excitement,
 everyone in The Beautiful Garden cried:

Colorful Rainbow Butterfly,
Please come out and don't be shy!

We want to hear what you have to say.
And we need for you to lead the way.

Colorful Rainbow Butterfly,
We really want to see you fly.

Spread your wings but let us know
What you've learned before you go.

Suddenly, a brightly colored butterfly appeared
and sang in the most beautiful voice:

I am the Rainbow Butterfly,
Here to greet you and say "hi."
Are you green, orange, purple or gray?
Don't be sad; you're okay.

        I am the Rainbow Butterfly
        Like you I used to sometimes cry.
        I felt alone and didn't belong
        'Til I learned I was wrong.

I am the Rainbow Butterfly.
When you see me flutter by,
Think how awesome you really are
Smile – you're a superstar!

        I am the Rainbow Butterfly
        With the colors of earth and sky.
        When you see me up above
        Think of your parents' love.

Then,

the Rainbow Butterfly

flew off to share her very special knowledge

about love with everyone who would listen.

For my multiracial, multicultural, and multicolored family,
whose beauty – inside and out – inspired this story.

For Angelica, a/k/a Esperanza,
who has been, is and forever will be my muse and *raison d'etre*.

ACKNOWLEDGEMENTS

To all my family and friends, thanks for your support and encouragement as I embark on my new venture as a children's illustrated books author.

To Santiago Cornejo and the other artists at Enroc Illustrations: You've done it again. Thank you.

And, of course, to Reagan Rothe and the entire team at Black Rose Writing, thanks for the wild ride.

ABOUT THE AUTHOR

A first-generation immigrant to the U.S. from the Philippines, Marissa Bañez is a graduate of Princeton University and a lawyer licensed to practice in New York, California and New Jersey. She has published legal articles for the prestigious *New York Law Journal* and the American Bar Association, but her true passion is writing children's stories that are designed to entertain as well as teach through both words and illustrations. Her first book is *Hope and Fortune*, whose main characters (Esperanza and the Fortune Fairies) make a cameo – but critical – appearance in *Hues and Harmony*. Marissa lives in New York City.

©2023 by Marissa Bañez
All rights reserved. No part of this book may be reproduced, stored in a retrieval system or transmitted in any form or by any means without the prior written permission of the publishers, except by a reviewer who may quote brief passages in a review to be printed in a newspaper, magazine or journal.

The author grants the final approval for this literary material.

First printing

This is a work of fiction. Names, characters, businesses, places, events, and incidents are either the products of the author's imagination or used in a fictitious manner. Any resemblance to actual persons, living or dead, or actual events is purely coincidental.

ISBN: 978-1-68513-237-8
PUBLISHED BY BLACK ROSE WRITING
www.blackrosewriting.com

Printed in the United States of America
Suggested Retail Price (SRP) $22.95

Hues and Harmony is printed in Papyrus*As a planet-friendly publisher, Black Rose Writing does its best to eliminate unnecessary waste to reduce paper usage and energy costs, while never compromising the reading experience. As a result, the final word count vs. page count may not meet common expectations.

We hope you enjoyed reading this title from:

www.blackrosewriting.com

Subscribe to our mailing list – *The Rosevine* – and receive **FREE** books, daily deals, and stay current with news about upcoming releases and our hottest authors.
Scan the QR code below to sign up.

Already a subscriber? Please accept a sincere thank you for being a fan of Black Rose Writing authors.

View other Black Rose Writing titles at www.blackrosewriting.com/books and use promo code
PRINT to receive a **20% discount** when purchasing.

CPSIA information can be obtained
at www.ICGtesting.com
Printed in the USA
JSHW040018260723
44549JS00002BB/44